我开始理解公鸡每天早起，然后尖叫

George Bernard Shaw

〔英〕萧伯纳 著

超人Cr 绘

潘韩婷 郭瑶 译

江苏凤凰文艺出版社
JIANGSU PHOENIX LITERATURE AND ART PUBLISHING

图书在版编目（CIP）数据

我开始理解公鸡每天早起，然后尖叫 / （英）萧伯纳(George Bernard Shaw) 著 ; 超人cr绘 ; 潘韩婷，郭瑶译. -- 南京 : 江苏凤凰文艺出版社，2025. 7. -- ISBN 978-7-5594-9840-3

Ⅰ. I561.065

中国国家版本馆CIP数据核字第202594NY68号

我开始理解公鸡每天早起，然后尖叫

〔英〕萧伯纳 著　超人 cr 绘　潘韩婷 郭瑶 译

责任编辑　项雷达
图书监制　古三月
选题策划　胡　杨
装帧设计　吉冈雄太郎
责任印制　杨　丹
出版发行　江苏凤凰文艺出版社
　　　　　南京市中央路 165 号，邮编：210009
网　　址　http://www.jswenyi.com
印　　刷　北京中科印刷有限公司
开　　本　787 毫米 ×1092 毫米　1/32
印　　张　7.75
字　　数　50 千字
版　　次　2025 年 7 月第 1 版
印　　次　2025 年 7 月第 1 次印刷
书　　号　ISBN 978-7-5594-9840-3
定　　价　58.00 元

目录

我开始理解公鸡
每天早起，然后尖叫

George Bernard Shaw

Part 1

我见过的鸡越多，就越喜欢打鸣

人生
唯一真正的
悲剧，

是发现自己
成了小人的
工具人。

我开始理解公鸡
每天早起，然后
尖叫

George Bernard Shaw

The only real tragedy
in life is the being
used by
personally minded men
for purposes
which you recognize to be base.

我不讨厌你，
但很烦你
听不懂
人话。

我开始理解公鸡
每天早起，然后
尖叫
George Bernard Shaw

I do not dislike you;

but

you bore me
when you
cannot understand.

人总幻想
为爱
对抗全世界，

结果
真的失去了
全世界。

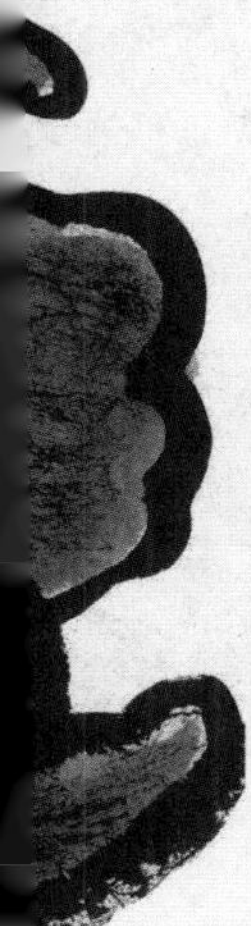

Men think
the world well
lost for them,

and
lose it
accordingly.

人越知羞耻，
就活得
越体面。

The more things
a man is ashamed of,
the more respectable
he is.

自由意味着责任，
这正是
多数人害怕它
的原因。

Liberty
means responsibility.
That is why most men
dread it.

好家伙！

物超所需，
必有烦忧。

The more a man possesses over
and
above what he uses,
the more careworn he becomes.

我们女人
一旦挑剔起男人的品格来，
就不用考虑
结婚这件事了。

If we women
were particular
about men's characters,
we should never get married at all.

家人同住时，
全靠滤镜保命；
家人不在时，
全靠吐槽续命。

When our relatives are at home, we have to think of all their good points or it would be impossible to endure them. But when they are away, we console ourselves for their absence by dwelling on their vices.

年轻人总被全世界谅解，
却不肯放过自己；

老年人总给自己找借口，
但没人愿意买账。

Youth,
which is forgiven everything,
forgives itself nothing:

age,
which forgives itself everything,
is forgiven nothing.

管你们是父子、夫妻
还是兄妹，
同居关系的真相
就是，

十分钟的假笑寒暄，
已是演技巅峰。

When two people live together—
it don't matter whether they're
father and son or husband
and wife or brother and sister—
they can't keep up the polite humbug
thats so easy for ten minutes
on an afternoon call.

我开始理解公鸡
每天早起，然后
尖叫

George Bernard Shaw

善与恶

并非泾渭分明——

二者你中有我，

我中有你。

People don't have their virtues
and vices in sets:
they have them anyhow:

all mixed.

爱恨本是双面胶，
当初贴得越紧，
现在就撕得越狠。

If you watch people carefully,
you'll be surprised to find how like hate is to love.

淑女和卖花女
之间的区别
不在于她做什么，
而在于别人说她什么。

The difference
between a lady and a flower girl
is not how she behaves,
but how she's treated.

我开始理解公鸡
每天早起，然后
尖叫

George Bernard Shaw

这世上没人能独善其身，
我们都应抱团取暖。

We are all dependent on one another,
every soul of us on earth.

如果一个人能意识到
活着本身就是幸福，
那他已经找到了
天堂。

That to live is happy,
has found his heaven.

我们这辈子
只会勤快地
“蛐蛐”他人，
自己却啥也不干。

We spend our lives
efficiently sneering at him
and doing nothing.

我开始理解公鸡
每天早起，然后
尖叫

George Bernard Shaw

当一个人
有秘密要倾诉时，
难的从来不是让他开口——
而是
如何让他闭嘴！

When a man has anything
to tell in this world,
the difficulty
is not to make him tell it,
but to prevent him from telling it
too often.

我开始理解公鸡
每天早起，然后
尖叫

George Bernard Shaw

天才都自带快乐属性，
面对任何苦难
都能勇往直前。

了这么多货!

There is
an irrepressible gaiety of genius
which enables it
to bear the whole weight
of the world's misery
without blenching.

打工人
打工魂

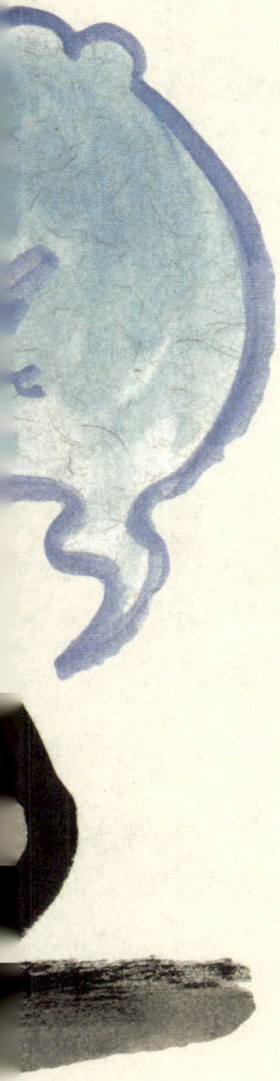

相信我，
动物也有灵魂，
同你我一样。
若天堂没有动物，
我宁可不去。

Oh,
believe me,
they have.
Just the same as you and me.
I really don't think
I could consent to go to heaven
if I thought there were to be no animals there.

不幸的家庭

是糟糕的育儿所。

An unhappy household is a bad nursery.

那些尝过婚姻甜头的人，
总会再次结婚。

People who have married happily once
always marry again.

两禽相悦

人类为找借口
能甩锅八百次，
能诉说一千种苦衷，
能卖惨一万种剧情，
唯独不敢承认
自己怂！

Man gives every reason
for his conduct save one,
every excuse for his crimes save one,
every plea for his safety save one;
and
that one is his cowardice.

我开始理解公鸡
每天早起，然后
尖叫

George Bernard Shaw

男女成年的**首要责任**是**发表**独立宣言。

The first duty of manhood and womanhood
is a Declaration of Independence.

上下级关系中
没有以礼相待可言。

The relation of superior
to inferior excludes good manners.

当心那些
打不还手的狠人——
他们不原谅你，
更不让你
原谅自己。

Beware of the man
who does not return your blow:
he neither forgives you
nor allows you
to forgive yourself.

我开始理解公鸡
每天早起，然后
尖叫

George Bernard Shaw

自我感动的戏码
演足了，
让别人牺牲
也成了理所当然。

Self-sacrifice enables us
to sacrifice other people
without blushing.

我开始理解公鸡
每天早起，然后
尖叫
George Bernard Shaw

如今最精于筑巢的生物，
生来既无甲壳护体，
亦无毛羽蔽身。

The most elaborately housed beings today
are born not only without houses
on their backs
but without even fur
or feathers to clothe them.

我开始理解公鸡
每天早起，然后
尖叫

George Bernard Shaw

要是进步能成真，
那人类向善的念头
总得压过向恶的冲动吧！

我开始理解公鸡
每天早起，然后
George Bernard Shaw
尖叫

点进步

If progress were a reality,
his beneficent impulses must be gaining
on his destructive ones.

生命不分贵贱，
都值得被救。

A man's life is worth saving,
whoever it belongs to.

我开始理解公鸡
每天早起，然后
尖叫
George Bernard Shaw

加油！

人人都不一样，
你我皆是
人间限量版。

We are not all the same,
any more than you are.

我开始理
每天

Part 2

当你停止笑时，你就会变老

人生

有两大扎心事：

一是得不到想要的，

二是得到了想要的。

Here are two tragedies in life.
One is not to get your heart's desire.
The other is to get it.

如果为了钱
要不停打工，
那
有再多钱又有何用？

What is the use of having money
if you have to work for it?

太卷了!

不要按自己喜欢的方式
对待他人——
人家的喜好可跟你不一样。

Do not do unto others as you would
that they should do unto you.
Their tastes may not be the same.

社会！
盲目

金科玉律第一条：
世上没有金科玉律。

爬到顶也没用……

The golden rule is that there are no golden rules.

对就是对，
错就是错——
分不清的人非蠢即坏，
没第三种选项。

Right is right;
and wrong is wrong;
and if a man cannot distinguish them properly,
he is either a fool or a rascal: that's all.

哦耶！

醉鬼船长
总指望老天庇佑，
却不知
老天最爱看他们
触礁。

Every drunken skipper trusts to Providence.
But one of the ways
of Providence with drunken skippers
is to run them on the rocks.

我开始理解公鸡每天早起，然后尖叫

George Bernard Shaw

你的常识

还不如一只呆鹅。

You' ve no more common sense
than a gander.

我曾给过你整个银河系，
现在却要我
帮你缝衣拖地？

I gave you eternity
in a single moment.
Must I mend your clothes
and sweep your floors as well?

生活不会因为有人死去

就失去趣味，

就像

它不会因为有人欢笑

就失去严肃一样。

Life does not cease to be funny
when people die any more
than it ceases to be serious
when people laugh.

爱是通天火，
笑傲阎王座！

Love that illumines,
laughing at Death.

当生命结束时，
艺术才真正开始。
年轻时我们投身艺术，
却不知所以；
只有当我们
走完这一程才明白，
代价是错过了生命本身。

Where life ends, Art begins.
In youth we turn to Art,
we know not why;
and only when we have gone through with Art
and come out on the other side,
we learn to our cost that we have missed Life itself.

没有女人能熬了通宵
还容光焕发。

禁止

我开始理解公鸡
每天早起，然后
尖叫
George Bernard Shaw

“耶”！

No woman looks her best
after sitting up all night.

理想婚姻是偶像剧，
现实婚姻是纪实片。

不太
啊……

Marriage as a fact is not in the least
like marriage as an ideal.

我要想的事情还有很多，
跟你闲聊
简直是浪费生命。

I have so much to think of.
This chat of ours
seems to me an unbearable waste of time.

我命由我不由天，
无须外界插手。

Human life,
is the only thing that takes care of itself.

每个梦都是预言，
每个玩笑
都暗藏深意。

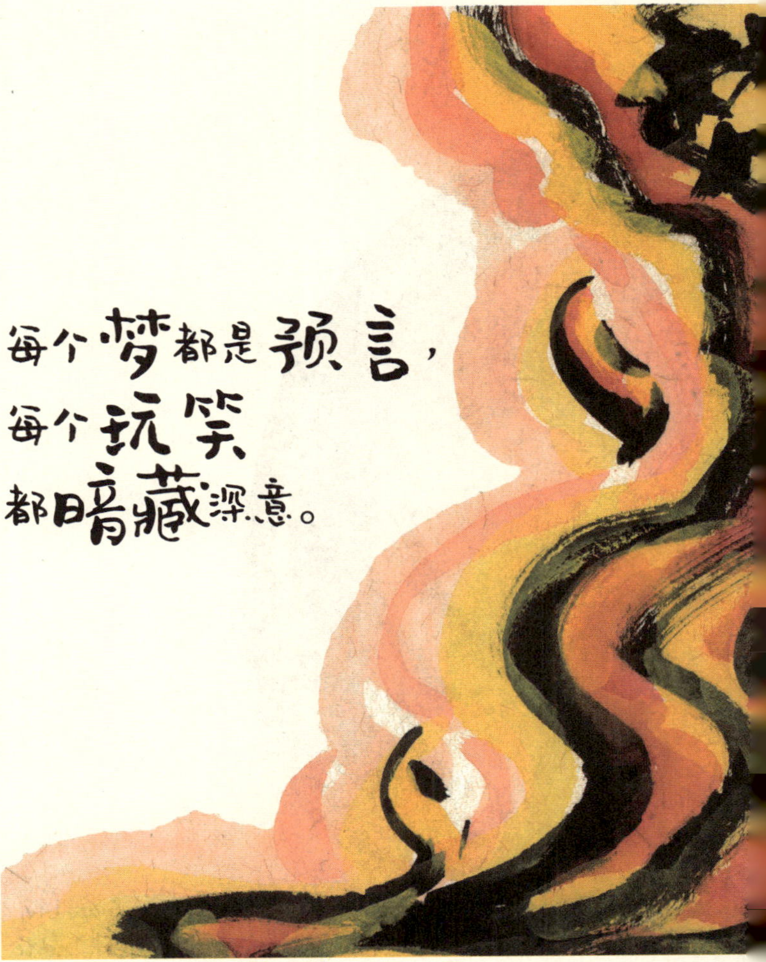

Every dream
is a prophecy:
every jest is an earnest
in the womb of Time.

痛苦的来源就是，
你有闲工夫
去纠结自己是否快乐。

The secret of being miserable
is to have leisure to bother
about whether you are happy or not.

真不容易啊！

纠结过得舒不舒坦
只会让生命
失去存在的意义。

我开始理解公鸡
每天早起，然后
尖叫

George Bernard Shaw

Life
is not worth living
if you have to bother
about comfort.

世间最真诚的爱，
莫过于对美食的爱。

There is no love sincerer
than the love of food.

生命原力令我臣服：
抱住你的时候，
我便拥有了整个世界。

The Life Force enchants me:
I have the whole world
in my arms
when I clasp you.

我开始理解公鸡每天早起，然后尖叫

George Bernard Shaw

我在故我思。

I am;
therefore I think.

每天坚持写日记……

地狱由善意

而非恶意铺就——

毕竟人人都自认心怀好意。

Hell is paved with good intentions,
not with bad ones. All men mean well.

所谓
“有好身体才有好脑子”
就是胡说八道，
应该是
有好脑子才能有好身体。

Mens sana in corpore sano is a foolish saying.
The sound body
is a product of the sound mind.

我开始理解公鸡
每天早起，然后
尖叫

George Bernard Shaw

如果历史不断重演，
意外也总在发生，
人类该有多不善于
从经验中学习啊！

If history repeats itself,
and the unexpected always happens,
how incapable must Man be of learning
from experience!

生活如此，
该咋办就咋办。

Life is what it is;
and I am prepared to take it as it is.

我开始理解公鸡
每天早起，然后
尖叫

George
Bernard
Shaw

生活哪有什么阴暗面——
它本就是一个整体。

There is no wicked side:
life is all one.

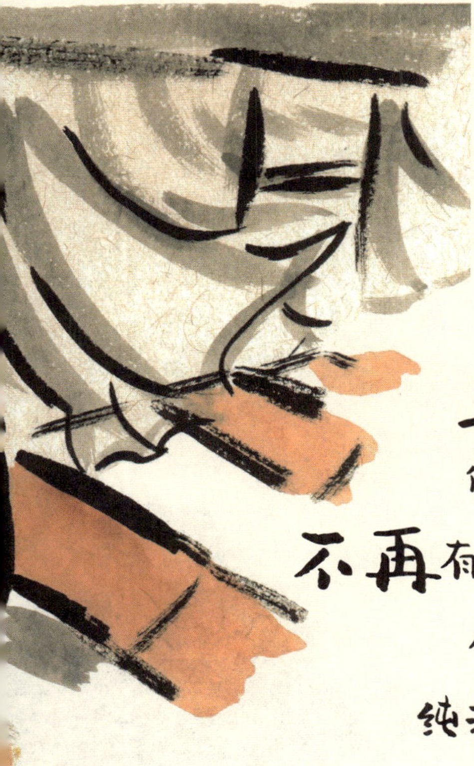

人老了，
身心的容器
便干涸了，
不再有汹涌的澎湃，
人又变回了
纯洁的孩子。

In old age
the vessel dries up:
there is no overflow,
you are a child again.

什么都没有发生，
除了
不值一提的
小事。

Nothing happens,
except something
not worth mentioning.

我开始理解公鸡
每天早起，然后
George Bernard Shaw
尖叫

「ye」孩子
凯

岁月催人老，
成熟周周新。

Growth is too rapid
at my age:
I am maturing
from week to week.

家教的最大难题：

让家人在自家客厅的体贴度，

追上在别人家做客时的

殷勤劲儿。

The whole difficulty
of bringing up a family well
is the difficulty of making its members
behave as considerately at home
as on a visit in a strange house.

总有一个**倒霉蛋**

要当牙医第一次实操的

小白鼠。

Every dentist
has to begin on somebody.

Part 3

开始理解公鸡
每天早起，然后
尖叫

George Bernard Shaw

未来取决于梦想
所以赶紧睡觉去

在这个世界上
取得成功的人，
是那些主动
寻找机会的人；
如果找不到，
就自己创造。

The people who get on
in this world are the people
who get up and look for
the circumstances they want,
and,
if they can' t find them,
make them.

大风大浪
超人CR是个人才!

没有主张，

何来风格？

He who has nothing to assert
has no style
and can have none.

我开始理解公鸡
每天早起，然后
尖叫

George Bernard Shaw

……不能在一个地方待着……

人生真正的快乐
只有一种：
被自己认准的目标
追着跑，
根本停不下来。

The true joy in life,
the being used for a purpose recognized
by yourself as a mighty one.

别抗拒**诱惑**，
尝遍天下鲜，
可真香！

我开始理解公鸡
每天早起，然后
尖叫
George Bernard Shaw

品学「煎贝」

Never resist temptation:
prove all things:
hold fast that which is good.

要努力争取
你想要的，
否则
你只能被迫接受
你得到的。

Take care to get
what you like
or
you will be forced to like
what you get.

能者行之，
不能者教之。

He who can,
does.

He who cannot,
teaches.

我开始理解公鸡
每天早起，然后
尖叫

George Bernard Shaw

正常人死磕自己，
轴人魔改世界——
人类进度条
全由轴人加载。

The reasonable man adapts himself
to the world:
the unreasonable one persists
in trying to adapt the world to
himself.
Therefore all progress
depends on the unreasonable man.

我开始理解公鸡每天早起，然后尖叫

George Bernard Shaw

爱时
掏心又掏肺，
恨时
反噬成累赘。

If you begin
by sacrificing yourself to those
you love,
you will end
by hating those to whom
you have sacrificed yourself.

我开始理解公鸡每天早起，然后尖叫

George Bernard Shaw

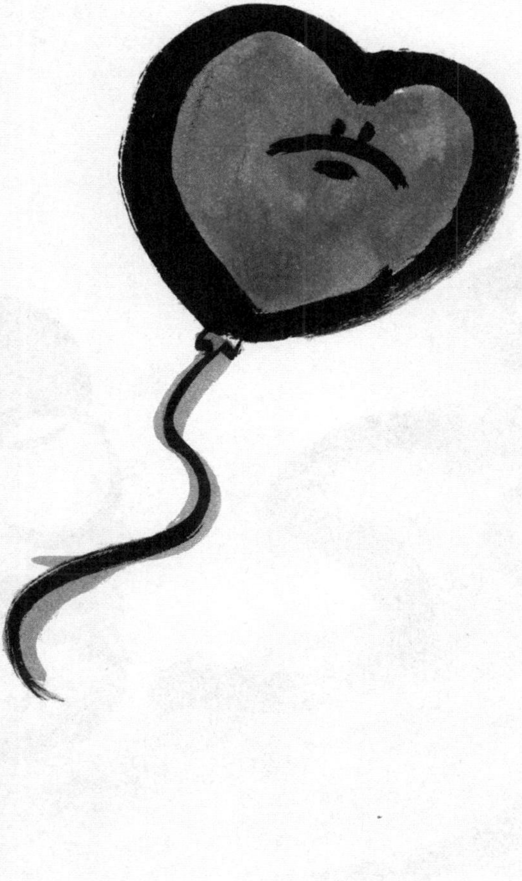

选好自己要走的路，
并坚持到底。

It's better to choose your line
and go through with it.

心无挂碍，

万般自在。

When you
want nothing,
you can
do anything.

能把爱好
当饭碗的人
简直是人生赢家！

Happy is the man
who can make a living
by his hobby!

力量的钥匙
是什么？
答案就是——
我信自己！

What is the secret
of your power?
Only that
you believe in yourself.

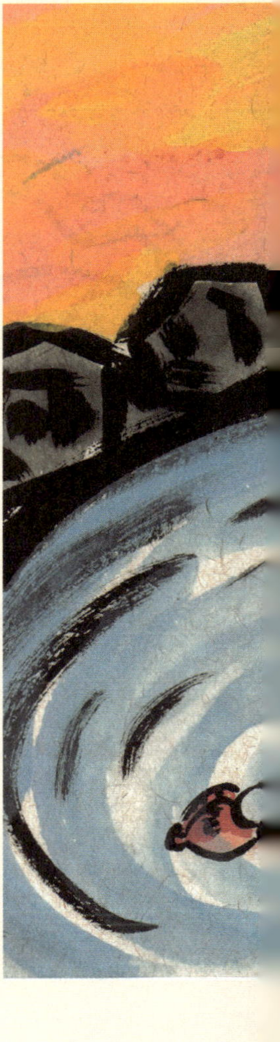

我开始理解公鸡
每天早起，然后
尖叫

George Bernard Shaw

富鸡清醉

幸福于我如鸡肋，
光盯着糖罐子，
哪还有劲儿做自己？

Happiness is the most tedious thing
in the world to me.
Should I be what I am
if I cared for happiness?

英雄也有软肋。

Even the bravest man fears something.

我开始理解公鸡
每天早起，然后
尖叫

George Bernard Shaw

真正的困难
是不让人们做无用功，
而要花心思让他们发现
自己真正热爱且擅长的事。

The real difficulty
is to prevent them from wasting their time
by reading for the sake of reading
and studying for the sake of studying,
instead of taking some trouble to find out
what they really like and are capable
of doing some good at.

头

请记住，
世界的进步
取决于你比长辈
懂得更多。

Remember that
the progress of the world
depends on your knowing better
than your elders.

蛋定

自律的终极目标——
驾驭自我。

The greatest of these is self-control.
The final objective of this Will was power over self.

活得久不如活得透——
让你在意的
不应该是
活了多少年，
而是
还剩多少天。

It is not the number of years
we have behind us,
but the number we have before us,
that makes us careful and responsible and determined
to find out the truth
about everything.

大自然是治疗
世间一切疾病的
真正解药。

The true remedy
for all diseases
is Nature’s remedy.

活力与勇气
是女性最珍贵的特质，
而母性
则是她迈向成熟的
庄严起点。

我开始理解公鸡
每天早起，然后
尖叫
George Bernard Shaw

Vitality and bravery
are the greatest qualities
a woman can have,
and motherhood her solemn initiation
into womanhood.

身处地狱者
随波逐流，
身处天堂者
掌舵航行。

To be in hell is
to drift,
to be in heaven is
to steer.

帆少年

实践
是获取知识的
唯一途径。

Activity
is the only road
to knowledge.

美德

不在于克制恶行，

而在于

不生恶念。

Virtue consists,
not in abstaining from vice,
but in not desiring it.

我们必须学会直面死亡——
学会从真正意义上
理解死亡的含义。
怕死，
是人世间一切冷漠的根源。

We must learn to die,
and to die in the fullest sense
of the word.
The fear of the end
is the source
of all lovelessness.

我开始理解公鸡
每天早起，然后
尖叫

George Bernard Shaw

重要的

不是最终说了算，

而是

从自己的方式

达成目的。

我开始理解公鸡
每天早起，然后
尖叫

George Bernard Shaw

The important thing
is not to have the last word,
but to have your own way.

勇敢

不会因付出些许痛苦

而减损其价值。

Bravery

is none the worse

for costing a little pain.

我开始理解公鸡
每天早起，然后
尖叫

George Bernard Shaw

要在世上立足，
靠的不是
消极防守，
而是
主动出击——
哪怕被打得
头破血流。

You don't learn to hold your own
in the world by standing on guard,
but by attacking,
and getting well hammered yourself.

我的身体是尘土，我的灵魂不是。我的身体由什么构成重要吗？地上的尘土、空气中的微粒，甚至是沟渠里的污泥？无论它是什么，重要的是，当造物主将生命的气息吹入这具身体，它就成了有灵魂的人。

My body is dust, not my soul. What does it matter what my body is made of? the dust of the ground, the particles of the air, or even the slime of the ditch? The important thing is that when my Creator took it, whatever it was, He breathed into its nostrils the breath of life; and Man became a living soul.

我们的思想无非是对自我的认知；而任何增添这种认知的人，都是在创造新的思想，正如孕育新生命一样确定无疑。

Our minds are nothing
but this knowledge of ourselves:
and he who adds a jot to such knowledge creates new
mind as surely as any woman creates new men.

真正的原创风格从不为风格本身而存在。

A true original style is never achieved for its own sake.

我开始理解公鸡
每天早起，然后
尖叫
George Bernard Shaw

勤俭
是一切美德的根源。

The love of economy
is the root of all virtue.

Part 4

我开始
每天

George
Berna
Shaw

用荒诞对抗荒诞，

叫鸡
然后
叫

用尖叫回应尖叫

智慧
不是靠经验堆成的——
要不然化敦的每一块石头，
都该比牛津教授更聪明。

If we could learn from mere experience,
the stones of London would be wiser
than its wisest men.

世间万物皆受限，
故世间无物能自由。

Nothing
can be unconditional,
consequently nothing
can be free.

对人最大的恶，
不是恨，
而是不在乎——
冷漠才是彻底丧失人性的
表现。

The worst sin towards our fellow creatures is not to hate them, but to be indifferent to them: that's the essence of inhumanity.

人生不就是由
一连串富有灵感的蠢事
组成的吗？
难的是
怎么去付诸实践。
别错过任何机会：
它不会每天都来。

What is life
but a series of inspired follies?
The difficulty
is to find them to do.
Never lose a chance:
it doesn't come every day.

我开始理解公鸡
每天早起，然后
尖叫

George Bernard Shaw

如果
我们真的明白
自己在做什么，
还会去做吗？

Do any of us understand
what we are doing?
If we did, would we ever do it?

我开始理解公鸡
每天早起，然后
尖叫

George Bernard Shaw

所有人都崇拜
真理、纯洁
与无私，
原因如出一辙——
因为他们都在
叶公好龙。

Everybody worships truth,
purity, unselfishness,
for the same reason—
because they have no experience
of them.

一个人

若连这点**钱**都挣不到，
还谈什么

结婚和**体面**？

How is the man
to marry and live a decent life
on less?

我开始理解公鸡
每天早起，然后
尖叫

George Bernard Shaw

世上只有
妈妈好
多福

唯有成年人的
善意与良知
可以
保护儿童。

The child has no defence in any case
except the kindness and conscience
of the adult.

孩子理应四处闯荡，
因为
他本就该
四海为家。

我开始理解公鸡
每天早起，然后
尖叫

George Bernard Shaw

A child should wander
because it ought to be at home
everywhere.

艺术是虚妄的，
唯有生活是真实的。

Art is false
and life alone is true.

学艺术
是需要很多的
你家的条件……

我也知道
不可能。

所有职业都是外行人眼中的阴谋。

All professions are conspiracies against the laity.

养天才的钱够他们活命就行，
但想买他们的良心
可是另外的价钱。

If a man' s a genius,
you want to pay him enough to keep him alive;
but you can' t pay him enough to keep him honest.

艺术家要么是诗人，
要么是无赖：
作为诗人，
他看不清现实……
作为无赖，
他看不见混吃等死、
乞讨、撒谎和吹嘘的
代价。

The artist is either a poet
or a scallawag:

as poet,
he cannot see,
as the prosaic man does,
that chivalry is at bottom only romantic suicide;

as scallawag,
he cannot see that it does not pay to spunge
and beg and lie and brag.

将婚姻与道德
混为一谈
是对人类良知的
终极破坏。

The confusion of marriage
with morality
has done more to destroy
the conscience of the human race
than any other single error.

我开始理解公鸡每天早起，然后尖叫

George Bernard Shaw

当平等无可争议时，
服从亦如是。

Where equality is undisputed,
so also is subordination.

人猎杀老虎时
称为乐趣，
老虎袭击人
却被称为暴行——
罪行与正义的界限
不过如此。

When a man wants to murder a tiger
he calls it sport:
when the tiger wants to murder him
he calls it ferocity.
The distinction between Crime and Justice
is no greater.

无知之处，
愚昧便自封为科学。

Where there is
no knowledge ignorance calls
itself science.

当我愚昧时，想做什么就做什么……如今我变聪明了，却连顾及自身的时间都没有。

When I was foolish,
I did what I liked...
Now that I am wise,
I have no time to attend to myself.

孩子被教导
要善良、恭敬、安静，
不能顶嘴……
最重要的是服从，
要“只被看见，不被听见”。

The child is taught to be kind,
to be respectful,
to be quiet, not to answer back...
to be above all things obedient,
and to be seen and not heard.

公正就是不站队
——唯有局外人
才能真正做到。

Justice is impartiality.
Only strangers are impartial.

口头承诺
永远不如白纸黑字可靠，
毕竟话说了会忘，
但字迹可以永存。

Your word can never be
as good as your bond,
because your memory can never be
as trustworthy as your honor.

在愚昧的国度，
天才被奉若神明——
人人崇尚膜拜，
无人听其指引。

In a stupid nation
the man of genius becomes a god:
everybody worships him
and nobody does his will.

我开始理解公鸡
每天早起，然后
尖叫

George
Bernard
Shaw

当小孩的隐藏关卡：
学不懂的定理，
躲不过的雷区。

The consequence of being a child is
that you cannot understand
what you are being forced to learn,
nor what you are being protected from.

我开始理解公鸡
每天早起，然后
尖叫

George Bernard Shaw

男人不会爱上所有女人，
女人也不会爱上所有男人。
大部分时候，根本不会
看对眼。

No man ever fell in love with the entire female sex,
nor any woman with the entire male sex.
We often do not fall in love at all.

男人就像一台
只有六张唱片的留声机，
你听到耳朵长茧还得坐在桌边，
看他对着每位新访客按下播放键。

A man is like a phonograph
with half-a-dozen records.
You soon get tired of them all;
and yet you have to sit at table
whilst he reels them off to every new visitor.

从年少天真
到看透世故
通常需要十五年。

The process of growing
from romantic boyhood
into cynical maturity
usually takes fifteen years.

说明——

本文句子选自萧伯纳以下作品

《人与超人》《革命者的箴言》《卖花女》《恺撒和克丽奥佩特拉》
《心碎之家酒店》《芭芭拉少校》《华伦夫人的职业》《回到马土撒拉》
《魔鬼的门徒》《另一个岛屿》《十四行诗中的黑暗女士》《安德罗克里斯和狮子》
《结婚》《医生的困境》《完美的评论》《命运之人》《父母与孩子论》
《你永远无法判断》《她如何对她的丈夫撒谎》